THE DEVIL'S CITY

SARA TANTLINGER

MATT CORLEY

saturday morning scenarios, llc
saint louis, mo

Praise for The Devil's City

"*The Devil's City* is a helluva thrill ride, delving deep into the sick history of serial killer HH Holmes, brutally peeling back the layers of his evil legacy through a series of surprising character studies, viciously unraveling Holmes' evil blood lust, victim after victim, until it reveals an unexpected core lurking behind it all. Holmes experts Sara Tantlinger and Matthew Corley have built a whole new underworld around the killer's infamous Murder Castle at turn of the century Chicago, and this book takes you straight down into the twisted intricacies its darkest abyss. LOVED IT."

—Michael Arnzen,
Bram Stoker Award-winning author of *Play Dead*

"In *The Devil's City*, Sara Tantlinger & Matt Corley have created a phantasmagoric fun house of a novel, heavy on the gore. The novella takes the story of H.H. Holmes and gives it an even darker twist. A suspenseful, highly recommended read."

—John F.D. Taff,
Multiple Bram Stoker Award Nominee, author of *The Fearing*

"Time and time again I'm rooting for the victims and feeling sad at their ghastly deaths. They are all so believable and I want them to somehow escape the clutches of the owner of the 'Murder Hotel'. Really creepy, really evocative noir horror."

—Lee Carnell, The Dholehouse.org

Paul Grodzka

The boy is vexing. Silent, stoic, and covered in the grime of menial labors. The invasions into my waking thoughts and fitful slumbers come with urgent frequency. Enticing and appalling at once. Calling to memory Francis, my most intimate of friends from university. Perhaps that's the impetus of my fascination? Yearning to see my Canadian mate after all these years? My bodily state when rousing from the dreams is most intense. Pitezel watches the lad in my stead, and I lay in wait until I can abstain no longer. It is most invigorating.

—From the diary of HH Holmes

PAUL DOESN'T MIND the rough, mindless work. It allows his thoughts to wander. To lose himself in times gone by when everything was different. Before coming to America. Before momma got sick. Before even, the Littles were born, when days were filled with excitement, dreams, and wonder.

"Move ya ass Paul!"

With a nod to Mr. Pitezel he tosses the tobacco stub, finishes loading the rough, grey blocks, and wheels them into the partially constructed hotel for the bricklayers. By end of day the discharged bricks had been stacked, the process repeated dozens of times, and the bone-weary exhaustion of a day's hard labors settles in.

A half dozen languages fill the air from the workers' chatter. Mr. Holmes' isn't particular about who he hires, though few stay on more than a few weeks. Scraps of German, French, Chinese, and his native Polish came to Paul's ears. As always, he gives no sign of understanding. Truth be told the workers have come to the near unanimous conclusion that he is simple. That said, he works hard,

1

literally asks for nothing, and the only sign of his presence is the pungent smell of cheap tobacco clinging to Paul from the ubiquitous hand rolled cigarette in his mouth.

The lake wind eddies cool the workers, carrying away the odors of the unwashed men and their habits. It's unseasonably hot for Chicago in October; a chill settles over Paul nonetheless and he hunches his shoulders, curling in upon himself to keep what little warmth his slight body has.

"Mister P, we gettin' paid today?" Paul's eyes raise to better see the man, a head shorter and hunched from long days of labor, questioning the foreman. The laborer's harsh brogue identifies him as an Irishman. He's new, coming on just a few days ago, and already grumbling about late pay.

Glaring, Pitezel wilts the slighter man. The rictal grin on Pitezel's face is enough to cause him to take an involuntary step back. A step too short, too late, to prevent the jackhammer blow to his jaw from dropping him to the floor. A pair of workers move to lift the Irishman, but not before Pitezel delivers a vicious kick to his downed victim's kidneys eliciting a fresh groan of pain.

Throughout it all Paul stands apart, watching with implacable disinterest, a half-spent cigarette, and gratitude that he's made it one more day without calling any attention to himself. Or so he thought.

"Mr. Holmes has a job that needs done tonight. It's your lucky day." The faintest of smiles lifted the corners of Pitezel's mouth, as if he'd made a joke.

"And put that shit out."

The path the men take is familiar, as it's the same route Paul travelled countless times today in delivering bricks to the masons. Dust, webs, and debris are everywhere. Typical for a construction site. Stopping at particularly large heap deep within the innards of the hotel, Pitezel looks back at Paul.

"Clean this mess. Any idiot could do it, so's you should be fine. Finish tonight and . . . " the flash of a quarter is all the incentive needed.

The Littles will be fine if I'm a bit late. I'll make it up to them with something better than two-day old bread.

With a nod Paul begins his labors, already imagining the bread, potatoes, and stew meat he'll be bringing home. Paul retreats into the depths of his mind. Dirt, detritus, and debris removed the room is cleaned. Exhausted, it takes longer than expected, but with mindless resolve it gets done, leaving Paul in the dimly lit room, near shaking, and muscles spent.

Pitezel steps softly with purpose and poise. This isn't his first hunt in the hotel. He stays to the shadows, avoiding obstacles and creaky sections of floor with ease until he's behind his victim, saturated rag at the ready.

The men—Pitezel larger, stronger, and with the element of surprise—struggle for mere moments. Strong arms encase the smaller man's chest, there's a brief hesitation as Pitezel's hands feel an unexpected softness, but Paul's stupefied reaction to the assault does nothing to stop the hand snaking upward with a damp cloth. The folded handkerchief covers Paul's mouth filling it with an unfamiliar sweet tang, and invading his nostrils with an overwhelmingly dense, penetrating vapor.

Pitezel holds his prey tightly until all doubts of the chloroform's effectiveness have been eliminated. With surprising gentleness, Paul is set down, placed in the waiting barrow, and carried deeper into the labyrinthine hotel.

"I'll be damned. No wonder the boss wanted this one so bad."

Senseless, Paul's mind withdraws reliving the day of his birth.

A woman, skin shiny and taut to near bursting from the dropsy that plagued her, lay in bed covered by the worn, spidery thin blankets scavenged from their neighbors' refuse bins. She shares the room with her children, a young woman and fraternal twins whose malnourished bodies made their age difficult to gauge. The twins, a boy and girl with wet eyes, are holding hands, confused. Not so much by their momma, she'd been sick nearly as long as they could remember, but by their sister's garb.

"I have to find work, and this is the only way." The words are stilted, uncertain, and unmistakably tinged with excitement despite the dire circumstance. Momma insists on English at home, her foresight uncanny as always, and her voice worries over the unfamiliar words.

The canvas trousers, over-sized boots, and roughly sewn shirt are ill-fitting, grimy, and worn. And yet they feel right somehow. Freeing, despite the scandal it would cause she were to be found out. Raising to full height before the Littles stood Paul, their protector, their savior. He carried the weight of responsibility well, finding strength he'd not known was there, and feeling at peace with his path.

Looking back to the twins, "Remember, and this is very important, my name is Paul. I'm your wujek. Momma's youngest brother from Warsaw come to take care of you."

Mavis and Taavi nodded solemnly, and with the utter acceptance of the innocent welcome their uncle to the family.

Paul's emergence to consciousness is filled with disorientation and confusion. The room is much too warm to the be the hovel he shares with the Littles. That room, with its paper-thin walls, peeling paint, and drafty doors may as well be outside for the protection it gives. Gone too are the enveloping sounds of the city; the threads of light seeping through the porous walls and soft snores of the youngsters.

Aggressive silence and heavy darkness fill Paul's now racing heart with dread.

"Mavis, Taavi? Dzieci?"

The words pain him as much from disuse of his voice and the constant barrage of nicotine laden smoke to his throat as the mordacious chloroform he's now shaking off. The faint echo of his words returns to him, bringing with it the memory of unexpected attack.

Paul pushes himself up from the prone position he lay in, and in doing so notices the greasy, gritty dust beneath him. The purity of the all-encompassing darkness is disorienting; without thought Paul finds his matches, lights one, and the small room reveals itself to him. The coal cellar is empty save the omnipresent dust embedded in the walls, and blanketing the floor. Its only features are a chute in the ceiling, well out of Paul's reach, and the locked, nearly seamless door. Paul's skills of observation, perhaps blunted by the chloroform or growing sense of terror, were not up to the task of identifying the pair of five-fingered streaks on door left by the prior occupant.

Time loses meaning with his racing heartbeat, screams of anger, and pounding fists on implacable walls. Feeble blows against the door do little more than bruise Paul's hands. He worries at the seam succeeding only in tearing a fingernail from his blackened hands. Defeated the prisoner's anger is supplanted with fear; screams turn to wheezes from frantic exertion. Utterly spent, Paul sits in the darkness, knees drawn, leaning against the greasy wall, and unleashes his terror in a torrent of wracking sobs.

The craftsmen were utterly baffled by Holmes' insisting that the chutes required a locking mechanism. "A safety feature to ensure that the children don't crawl in and injure themselves," he insisted. Once installed they'd been oiled to be utterly silent.

Standing in the hallway Holmes smiled at his forethought. He marveled at his genius, and enjoyed the lamentations of his prisoner as if it were the finest French wine. When the cries subsided, Holmes left the corridor quoting a favorite poem in offering to an unseen presence,

"I'm sure you must be weary, with soaring up so high, will you rest upon my bed? said the spider to the fly."

In the darkness, Paul doesn't realize he's fallen asleep again, not until a soft, persistent susurrus nearby draws him from unconsciousness. He locates it easily in the quiet; three small holes each the width of his index finger issues a feeble exhalation of air. Paul worries at the openings in confusion and wonder, temporarily thinking of something other than the Littles and his confinement; the familiar pangs of withdrawal rush in as well. He thinks better with nicotine coursing through his body, and the comforting feel of a cigarette in his mouth.

Thankful for small blessings Paul's papers, tobacco, and matches are still in his pocket. With adept fingers and sure hands, rolling the cigarette in the dark was no challenge, he'd done it thousands of times. The ritual calms him, each practiced motion easing his anxiety. The sacrament ends with the application of fire to offering. Match flaring to life Paul catches a glimpse of a room denuded of all adornment. The concrete walls, floor, and ceiling are streaked with grime.

In the space between heartbeats, the meager light from the lucifer grows with a violent whoosh to an unbearable brightness. The volatile gas, trapped within the airtight room ignites with feverish intensity, white hot hellfire filling the room completely. Paul can't help but cringe, raising his hands for protection, shutting his eyes tightly against the onslaught, and the untouched cigarette falling in slow motion from his lips.

Eyebrows and the light dusting of hair on his arms combust in an instant. The startled gasp of recognition draws the raging flames into his nose, throat, and lungs; the unbearably intense pain triggers another, deeper inhalation, turning the world to white.

The tea set is cracked, mismatched, and missing a few necessary components, but to the little girl using it there is nothing finer in all of Warszawa. Delicate fingers place each spoon, plate, and cup just so on the crooked table. A setting for her, and another for her mama whose smiling face beams from across the table.

Mamuska's face reddens, blisters form, grow, and burst, as the chipped cup moves towards her mouth. Fissures of melting flesh run in rivulets, fingers turn to charred skeletal claws, and when the cup finally reaches her lips they sizzle from its heat. A flake of glowing ash floats away from the woman's raised pinky. Paulina's mama pays it no mind, continuing her teatime, losing more of herself with each moment until the teacup falls to the ground shattering, and she is nothing more than a film of greasy ash and char.

Little Paulina stares in horrific disbelief at her evanescing mother. The shock of seeing her momma, lost so long ago, provides the distraction and analgesia needed to discount her own predicament. All thoughts of the Littles flee her as she transports fully into the little girl she once was before the harsh realities of the world inadvertently led him to discover his truest nature. The cup cradled in her hands burns her flesh. The floating embers catch her dress and soft ringlets. She kneels forward, places herself in momma's lap, and surrenders to the consuming flames.

Victor Emory

The articulation process continues to escape my mastery. Chappell's teachings and expertise have been invaluable, but his knowledge is too mundane to meet my esoteric requirements. While he toils away to create specimens for the medical schools my creations will be so much more. My challenges notwithstanding, I will solve this riddle, and soon regardless of the efforts to which I must go.

I am bolstered by the beginnings of her encroachment. The workings ingrained in The Republic performed admirably. The masses do not see it as I do, not yet.

—From the Diary of HH Holmes

THE ARCHITECT BEAMED proudly at his sketched plans for the newest building. His crew would begin work immediately tomorrow on the foundation. Every inch of work would be a celebration to design, an ode to construction—he could not wait to show the director at once. Victor glanced around the hotel room, excited to share the plans with Lorelei. His wife of nearly twenty years sat straight-backed against a chair in the opposite corner of the room, a rather serious expression etched across her lovely face.

Victor was a prominent architect sent down from Pittsburgh by Mr. Burnham, Director of Works for the World's Fair, to assist with several projects as the city of Chicago geared up to host the World's Columbian Exposition. Victor found himself in several roles as the construction began—the organization was all over the place—and he had to shift his focus often, but it was a thrill. Each day brought something new, whether it was helping Burnham design those huge neoclassical buildings that were to be painted white, or directing workers on how to cast bronze lions for the Italian marble lobby.

9

The challenges excited him, and if he was honest with himself, took him away from Lorelei far too often. There were late nights where he could have gone back to the hotel in time to dine with her, but he chose to stay. To help make as much progress as possible because the stress and tension were beyond high to make this fair something truly unforgettable. If only he could convince Lorelei of this importance . . .

"My dear, please do not look so forlorn. Come here and see this creation!"

She shook her head. "No, Victor."

"What's wrong?" He sighed, feeling the enthrallment of the blueprints deflate beneath the gray cloud that followed Lorelei daily.

"I hate this city," she declared. "I hate your work. My very bones feel miserable in this place."

"Now, that's no way to be. The skeleton is the body's architecture. You must treat it more kindly."

"I hate when you say that! It's plain creepy. I was just telling . . . " she trailed off and crossed her arms.

"Telling who?" Victor shuffled out of the chair and away from the drawing desk.

"Nothing. I just met a new friend for tea yesterday and was remarking on how strange I thought your funny sayings were."

He inquired about this new friend, but Lorelei refused to say more; instead she pleaded that they go and have dinner together, after all Victor had come back to the hotel so late each day, they had not dined together for quite some time. She was right, and he could not refuse her this, so the subject was dropped, for now . . .

Lorelei had grown restless in her accompaniment of Victor to Chicago. Her city friends at home were off to finer places, country sides and beaches, but she'd made this whole affair sound as exciting as she could. *Yes, enjoy your trip,* she told her friends. *My Victor is going to build the World's Fair! The greatest fair any of us shall ever see in our lifetimes! Better than Paris.*

So she came with Victor, and she occupied herself as well as she could, but there was only so much for a woman to do in a place like this. And then one day she met a man who listened to her, who kept his wide eyes focused on her, and offered her something to give her purpose during this stay in Chicago.

Victor arrived back at the hotel earlier than usual thanks to a rain delay. After he settled himself in the room, Lorelei proudly exclaimed her news.

"Darling, I have found myself a job!"

At response to Victor's vacant expression and silence, she continued to explain about her new friend. A Mr. Henry Holmes who resided at the building locals had come to call "the Castle" in Englewood.

"My darling," Victor finally said. "You don't *need* a job. You are a well taken care of woman."

"I need a purpose, Victor. Something to do. And you know how I have an eye for diamonds and gems? Well, Henry spotted that in me right away. He asked about the emeralds I was wearing when we met, and we spoke in length about jewels and sales. It was most exciting."

"Oh, now he's *Henry,* eh?"

She sighed. "Don't be like that. I have been so restless, and now I can earn a little money for myself. What is so wrong with that?"

Victor left it alone at first. Let Lorelei have her job, it would only be temporary until this fair business was complete and then they could go back home, away from one sooty city and back to another, but it was their own place, at least.

But Lorelei's interest in the man, her new boss, kept growing. Victor knew something was off, but he refused to think it could have been anything more than . . . more than what?

Jealously traveled up Victor's body and settled like hot irons against his cheeks. His wife continued to pack her fine gowns in a fury of silken colors, stuffing each dress into her trunk rather than taking the time to fold the expensive material properly.

Exasperated, Victor sat on the edge of the bed at the Franklin's Hotel and pleaded for Lorelei to calm herself. "Please listen to me. You are not behaving rationally."

She huffed out a shaky breath and brushed dark red hair away from her face. The strands had come undone from her perfect updo and danced around her cheeks like wild flames. She paced around the room and another hairpin fell from her curls and onto the floor. Every last item she'd brought to Chicago was tucked away in the large suitcase.

"This god-forsaken place," she mused aloud. "*You* do not know what rational even is, Victor!"

He shot up from the bed and took a deep breath. The light blue of her eyes finally met his and he gently placed his hands on her shoulders.

"I love you. Does that mean nothing?"

She jerked away and then marched to the bed, quickly fastening the trunk securely. "You love your job more. I was a fool to come here."

He whispered her name and pleaded with her not to go. "I promise, I'll come home earlier when I can. Sometimes, I just can't."

Things were progressing well despite the rain, but recently there had been disasters, too. Shadows that loomed between constructing Burnham's fantasies to create the beautiful city of his dreams. Men fell from buildings to gory deaths below. Fires broke out. The grounds were not finished well in many areas and mud seeped everywhere, staining the dreamed-up "White City" in muck.

A girl vanished from a house just above Jackson Park where work was being done to create breathtaking scenery. Murder was nothing new, Victor realized, but the girl was only seventeen like his own daughter and the case deeply troubled him.

Yet all the workers pressed on. They had too, no matter their individual or collective troubles, and he needed Lorelei to press on, too.

The painful stabs of jealousy felt like he'd swallowed a thousand needles. Watching Lorelei ready herself to leave, to walk away without caring, was a loss of control he had never expected.

"Do as you please, Lorelei. I have a meeting with Burnham and this Mr. Tesla, just you wait and see what they're plotting. Once you come to the fair and see the grounds and buildings lit up in ways none of us have before, you'll understand what I've been doing. Why this project has been so important for me, for us."

She only shook her head and lingered in the doorframe of the cold hotel room. Dim light from the somber day filtered in through foggy windows. Victor felt like a pale ghost, watching the woman he loved ready to leave, wanting to reach out and touch her, stop her, but he just couldn't.

"Where will you even go?" Sadness turned his voice to a whisper.

"I . . ." she hesitated and refused to meet his gaze. "I have a room waiting."

"Where?"

"At the Castle. Mr. Holmes' building."

Victor's hands balled into shaking fists. "I bloody well know whose building it is, Lorelei! Absolutely not. I forbid you to stay or sleep anywhere near that man. He is poisoning us."

She sighed and a gentleness warmed her eyes for a moment. "You have been so oblivious, my husband. He was not the one to poison us." And with that she turned around, walked out the door, and did not turn back.

The next day was followed by more ruin and disaster. Something went wrong within a new building's design; more specifically, something Victor had tried to design . . .

He enjoyed clever tricks within buildings—things like a secret door when you pull on a candlestick levered into the wall, but a worker must have gotten the directions confused because now another worker had been crushed to death by the wall. The death was instant, but messy. The coats of paint needed to hide the man's blood on the walls, even after scrubbing everything as much as they all could, would set the project back several days.

Victor called it an evening and trudged back to the hotel. Let the others deal with their own incompetency.

The emptiness of the room reverberated within his own heart. Loneliness was truly a curse. He would find Lorelei, apologize like he should have done before, and plead for her return. He'd cut back some hours or make better efforts. Anything to get her away from that Holmes and his atrocious building . . . that castle. Victor imagined it must be poorly designed inside given the strange measurements he noticed on the outside when he had finally dared walk past it again.

He would find out.

The late afternoon sunk into chilled evening, and the Chicago winds sent the sharp smell of factory smoke across the streets where Victor briskly walked. He opened the door to the jewelry shop where a faint light glowed and expected to see Lorelei behind the counter, looking bored and relieved he had finally come for her.

Instead he found empty silence.

"Hello?" he called. "Lorelei?"

No answer.

No matter, he was a man on a mission. The layout of the place was strange, as if the curved walls and oddly placed staircases were initially meant to confuse and disorient visitors. But Victor understood the way a layout must go, even if it was meant to trick someone, there were only so many options in the end.

Upstairs, he found the doors to what must be the hotel rooms, but there was no way the rooms were even close to being filled. It was too quiet. The whole floor felt empty, like the shell of a place pretending to be something real.

Men like Holmes, Victor had seen them before. They were wealthy and figured they owned the world. Victor liked to think of his own success as something others could benefit from. He donated much back into the community and spent time with locals, though not as much time as he spent at work, and as he traversed the odd halls of this mad castle, he realized how often he spent time away from dear Lorelei.

After the children were grown and left for other opportunities, neither he nor Lorelei seemed to know what to do. They were still young enough, Victor figured, to enjoy things in this life. After all, people were living longer every day and pushing forty was a fine time to be prosperous and healthy with his beautiful wife.

He needed to tell her all of this, to apologize for the way he'd grown withdrawn from love. Let them leave this forsaken city and its dreams of white marble buildings for the silly fair all behind.

Not knowing what else to do, he yelled Lorelei's name in the middle of the hallway. He was not sure which room she might be in.

Again, only silence greeted him. No curious heads from other possible guests even poked out of their rooms to see what was happening. Distraught, he circled back and paced the hallway. A strange burst of cold air from what appeared to be a wall caught his attention. He placed a hand on the wall between the staircase and the archway that led to the rows of rooms. The wall was much colder here than elsewhere, as if something chilled were on the other side. A cellar room, maybe?

This wall, it must open, he realized. Something like what he had tried to create . . . something he hoped did not lead to death like it had for the worker. *What if Lorelei is down there, trapped in this man's basement?*

Frantically, he searched for a way to open the passage. At last he spotted it . . . a lantern affixed to the nearby wall that hung just an inch differently than the others. He pulled down on the black metal and the door disguised as a wall creaked open only enough to let a person squeeze through.

Did Holmes really think he was so clever that no one else could find this silly mechanism? No matter. Victor wasn't the strongest man in the world, but if this Holmes had hurt Lorelei in any way, he felt certain his rage would give him strength enough to do what must be done.

Carefully, he made his way down a curving set of stone stairs that led into darkness so deep, he could not see his hands in front of his face. Icy air drew out shivers from his body, and a rancid stench attacked his nostrils as he finally left the stairs and stepped into a dimly lit chamber.

The sour scent of death was something he'd encountered before. With slow steps, he traversed the winding corridor and found himself in a wide, concrete area where great vats lined the opposite wall. *Acid?*

Before he could inspect the tanks further, his eye caught a long figure covered by a dark cloth on the table toward the left side of the room. His heart kicked into overdrive from the fear, from the unexplained sense of *knowing* something horrible lay beneath that cloth.

Beyond the table, a great rack of sharp tools lay scattered. They looked like something a medieval torturer might use. Chains with metal handcuffs sprouted from bolts in the wall like brassy vines.

With shaking hands, he pulled back the cloth. A scream erupted from his throat the way a trapped, feral animal might burst from the cage once it has been freed. If the scream ever stopped, he was not sure.

Articulation, he was familiar with the word, the act of stripping flesh from bone. Lorelei's face was a soupy mess of liquid and flesh. Her body was only half-stripped of skin, while her other half lay naked and lifeless.

Dead, oh God. Lorelei.

Victor's entire body convulsed, sending a shock of bile to surge from his throat and onto the floor. His vision blurred and the room seemed to shrink around him. Madness ate at his brain like a flesh-eating worm.

He could not breath, yet he was aware of the growing shadow behind him. And he knew it must be Holmes, for whom else could such darkness belong to?

Victor stilled in front of the acid vat, staring down at it is vomit-green liquid, and he thought he heard it bubble and whisper to him. It told him not to fight this, for what was left to fight for without Lorelei?

Strong hands pushed Victor forward, causing him to lean his head down closer to the acid.

"You were right," the voice whispered, cold and smooth as a serpent.

Victor closed his eyes and tried to think of anything; the bronze lion statues, the plan for the White City, Lorelei dancing with him in her favorite blue dress . . . Lorelei's disfigured skeleton, dripping flesh, the ragged skin cut away inexpertly the way a rabid dog might tear a person apart.

"When you take away the flesh," the man continued and pushed Victor down further until his face was half an inch from the acid. "You really can see it—the beautiful architecture of one's body. Her skeleton, so lovely. I am afraid I have no time to pay you the same favor."

Rosine Van Tassel

The hotel continues to serve its purpose most admirably, as does my role as their apothecary. They see me as their trusted ally, dispenser of kindness, and as a gentleman whose only concerns are their wellbeing. I smile at the very thought of their misguided notions. The cattle in the stockyards know more of their fate than the strumpets who drawn to the web of comfort I've created, and the oblivion I sell in each bottle of my medicines.
                                            —From the diary of HH Holmes

THE WOMAN STEPPED gracefully through the crowded streets of Chicago, taking care to avoid the muck in the road leftover from spring rains and horse-drawn buggies. She slightly drew up her skirts as she navigated her way across unfamiliar territory.

She had meant to journey to Chicago for the great opening of the World's Fair, but some recent delay meant the fair was months away. No matter, she could easily stay in the city for that long and entertain herself. Her dear departed father left her in good standing, and the subsequent loss of her husband mere years later added to her wealth. He had been a well-known financial man sent on business to Ohio when a head-on collision with a freight train killed thirteen passengers.

She inhaled a deep breath and took a moment to enjoy standing on solid ground. The train ride had been smooth, but a dark terror lingered beneath her heart every time she traveled by train since her husband died. Anxious to rid herself of morbid thoughts, she took a brief rest at the hotel and then set about getting to know the city better. Dust from nearby factories covered the sky in brown vapors. A sooty tang stained the air, and it certainly was not the clean, country breeze she was used to, but she enjoyed the newness of exploring a place she'd never been to before.

Rosine was a strong woman, able to claim their estate and land without the hassle she initially expected. She journeyed to Chicago with hope of finding something or someone at the World's Fair worthy of investment. Without her husband and with no children of her own, helping someone out with their dreams appealed to her. She was not particularly gifted in conversation with strangers, but she was eager and independent, and liked the idea of being someone's benefactor. There was not much else to do these days, and she felt too old to pursue any silly dreams of her own.

The rich black of her dress collected mud near the hem; it was not a mourning dress, but ever since her husband's death, she found herself wearing dark colors every day. However, upon spotting the unmistakable architecture of the place she sought, she paid the dirt little mind. On her train ride over, the man across from her had spoken briefly of the building, remarking on it as a monstrous sight. His companion said he had never seen anything like it. As Rosine gazed upon the many windows and strange curving construction of the place, she agreed on the uniqueness of such a building, but found it exceptional and astounding rather than monstrous.

A line of shops made up the first floor, supporting the rooms on top, which Rosine assumed were some kind of apartments or a hotel. She entered the first door at the corner of Wallace and Sixty-third Street, taking note of the gold-plated plaque outside the shop that read, *Proprietor—H.H. Holmes.*

The widow left the bustle of Englewood behind and walked through the doorway of the quiet shop—a pharmacy. Shelves of both familiar and strange tonics, jars, herbs, and other promises lined the wall across from the windows. Sunlight yawned through the glass and caught particles of dust that swirled up from her dress and into the air.

At the counter stood a young woman with big eyes and a warm smile. Her fine dress was emerald green and she hardly looked like someone who needed a shop job to be supported.

"Good afternoon, madam," the girl said. "May I help you with anything today?"

Rosine smiled back, guessing the girl was barely twenty. "You lovely child, what are you doing in this dusty shop?" She walked closer and wondered if this girl could be the one she invested in; maybe she wanted to be an actress or a dancer, something silly and beautiful. Something Rosine wished she had done all those years ago while untethered by life's obligations.

"Tell me, if you could do anything, what would it be?"

Shyness crept onto the girl's features. She hesitated and then her eyes brightened, she opened her mouth—

"Emily?" A man's deep voice sounded from an office behind the counter.

The girl's smile wavered and she looked down, suddenly fascinated with smoothing out a wrinkle on her perfect dress.

"Emily," he repeated, calmer now. "Why don't you go finish going over the receipts? I will help this lovely lady."

The girl scrambled away, a crimson blush appearing on her fair cheeks. Rosine watched in curiosity, wondering if the girl was afraid of the man or emotionally attached to him. Perhaps there were more reasons than meets the eye of why she was here.

Rosine felt the man's attention on her immediately. Her own cheeks heated beneath the cold blue of his irises, such an intense gaze. The eyes weren't completely right, just a little cross-eyed, but he was a handsome man with fine features, and dressed exceptionally well. A small smile tugged at her lips as he bowed to her.

"How may I help you, my lady?" His voice was honey, and Rosine found herself leaning closer toward that sweetness.

His eyes flickered down her neckline for just a moment, but given the striking ruby necklace fastened around her throat, she wondered if he was glancing at the jewel or at something else.

"I'm afraid I have a bit of a toothache," she found herself saying, though it wasn't quite true. There was an ache somewhere within her, and she found herself desperate to just talk to the man. "Do you have anything that could help?"

"Of course." He shuffled past her with smooth movements, yet there was something skittery in that grace—an alertness attuned to his surroundings at all times. The man went behind his counter and carefully looked around, bringing out a small jar with a dropper.

"These drops will help, but don't overdo it," he warned her, the voice stern but there was a twinkle in those strange eyes.

He set the drops down and then held out a hand.

"Dr. Holmes, but please, call me Henry."

She shook the hand, surprised at its smoothness, and its chill. "Rosine Van Tassel."

His eyes widened. "Related to the late Edwin Van Tassel?"

She blinked in surprise. "Yes. He was my husband."

"I am sorry to hear that. I remember his name from the paper when that terrible crash happened. I had been following his investments for some time. He was a wise man with his stocks."

She smiled. "Indeed." Unsure of what else to say, she fidgeted with the thin lace of her gloves. Dr. Holmes, Henry, was more loquacious and filled the silence.

"I am terribly sorry. If you need anything Ms. Van Tassel, you let me know. Where are you staying? I have rooms here, you know."

Rosine blinked at the boldness of such a question. It was not common for a man to ask such things of a widowed woman, but something in his eyes excited her and compelled her to answer truthfully. "I'm staying with the Franklins, but I will be in town until the fair starts."

"The fair, of course. Well you can see how much closer my rooms are to the park. I promise you a view here unlike any other."

A laugh escaped her throat, and it was a rusty thing, unused for so long. "Are you always such a salesman, Dr. Holmes?"

The deep sapphire of his eyes twinkled. "Always."

Nearly three weeks had passed since Rosine moved her belongings into one of Henry's rooms within his labyrinth in Englewood. She tried every day to memorize the layout of the building, the way hallways twisted and curved, the disproportions of walls that made no sense, yet still the building stood in once piece without collapse. The place intrigued her, but also disoriented her without fail. There was a restlessness within this maze.

Tonight, her own restlessness came from an increasing worry in her mind that she had made a grave mistake. For the past three weeks, she had been continually charmed by Henry Holmes. They'd traveled around the city, gone shopping and bicycling through the spring air, had eaten at fine restaurants and delicate bakeries. She felt like a young girl again, being pursued by the great courting chase of a relationship.

He must have been at least five or six years her junior, but she was still a handsome woman after all, with enticing midnight hair and well-fitted dresses. She even retired her dark gowns and had accepted dear Henry's lavish gifts of silk dresses in assortments of colors. A bright green one made her think of the counter girl, Emily. She had apparently run off . . .

"She was terribly homesick," Henry had explained one afternoon when Rosine went looking for the girl, hoping to find a companion in this tangled web of a place.

"I sent her back on the train with enough money to cover the things she left here. She was so desperate to see her family again."

"Of course," Rosine agreed, but there was a heavy lurch in her gut.

A master of distraction, Henry had proclaimed himself to Rosine that same day. He kissed her in a passionate way that she would have deemed inappropriate of a suitor years ago, but he made it seem so delicious and welcome. The warmth spread through her like sunlight, and she never wanted to be apart from him. After supper, Henry confessed his dreams of expanding the hotel and shops attached, of hiring more employees and giving workers in need a chance to earn income.

"Do you not think the poor deserve such a chance? I would like to give them that opportunity, just as other men gave me opportunities long ago," he said, those blue eyes earnest despite their chill.

She had nodded, agreeing. "Perhaps I could help . . . "

It felt good to pledge her money to someone, and even though she'd only known the doctor a few weeks, it seemed like the right thing to do. The paperwork was drawn up in a whirlwind, and she found herself signing documents she barely looked over, for between kisses and warm caresses Henry would hand her another paper, a check, an agreement to something she did not take the time to comprehend.

And so restlessness followed her tonight, away from Henry's charm. Edwin would have had her head for being so foolish to sign papers and not read them thoroughly. He taught her much better than that, but the attentions of a charismatic man after so long of missing Edwin misguided Rosine, and she cursed herself for it.

She would sneak down to Henry's office, read over the files, and once her nerves were settled, she would find Henry himself and share his warmth tonight.

That was the lie she liked to tell herself.

Foolish woman. She shook her head and lit the dark blue kerosene lamp to guide her way. She left her stockinged feet bare, hoping it would help keep her quiet as a ghost. The layout of the upstairs rooms was a nightmare in the dim gloom of her small lamp. Walls jutted out where normal walls would not, and ancient paintings hung haphazardly from dark red wallpaper. She had tried to explore the place as much as possible, even rustling the knobs of locked doors, but Henry discouraged curiosity.

"Do you not think curiosity is adventurous?" she once asked him.

His serious eyes had locked on hers. "I think it dangerous."

She would not be dangerous tonight, merely cautious of what exactly she had signed away. The feeling of being swept up in love, she recognized its power. And alone tonight she finally started to think about the larger consequences of this man who seemed so good. Too good.

But maybe it was all in her head. She hoped it was, anyway. Wouldn't it be nice to find love instead?

Eventually she crossed through the labyrinthine layout of the upstairs and found the steps that led down to the offices.

The third stair from the bottom, she remembered. It had a terrible squeak. With careful poise she stretched over the step and past the dark shadows that followed her steps. Shadows that hunted her steps, if she only knew . . .

Her heart felt like a winged stone, heavy and beating rapidly, desperate to escape the cave of ribs holding it within her chest. A shaking hand reached toward the dark office door with Dr. H.H. Holmes written across its middle.

Creak.

She froze. The third step. *Who . . . ?*

She extinguished the lamp and shuffled away from the door, blind in the total darkness. She was certain she could navigate her way back to her room, but still did not want to be caught. There were only two other guests staying in Henry's apartment rooms that she knew of, at least that's what he said. She'd never actually seen them and just assumed they liked to be out in the city a lot.

A cold breath against the back of her neck sent a scream rocketing from her throat. It echoed so loud, surely someone would hear, would know. Surely Henry would come for her.

Heavy footsteps in the dark as the breathing thing shuffled away. She sprinted forward, colliding heavily with the body before tripping on the first stair. They fell together and she kicked away the grasping hands that felt like pincers around her ankles.

Rosine half crawled up the stairs in her frantic scramble, but she made it to the top without being caught. Henry's room was farthest down the hall, almost a straight shot except for the way the hallway curved. She calmed her breathing and used the wall to guide her, as quickly as she dared.

Her eyes adjusted a little to the dark, but not enough to make out anything concrete between the shadows. A whisper froze her body to the wall, like an arctic wind. Behind her, the horrible crunching of what sounded like bones cracking echoed down the hall. The very darkness itself seemed to grow. She backed up against a wall, her heart threatening to stop all at once with how hard it beat in her chest.

The shadow whispered her name and she screamed, but before she could move, the wall moved instead as if being rotated. Her very world tilted away and she not sure of anything other than the horrid stomach-flipping sensation of falling, and then sliding down a . . . was that a chute? In the hotel?

Rosine yelled out again into the darkness. Her screams echoed up the slick tunnel from where she fell, reverberating for no one to hear but the spiders who had built their webs within the darkness of a madman's castle.

Diana Stockman

I am unsure what disgusts me more. The newly created confectioners' abomination 'cracker jack' or that a flapdoodle would deign to masquerade as a woman to emasculate his betters. The gall to believe that a crowd of gentlefolk could be fooled by such vulgarity. Even the yokels from the country knew the trickery for what it was. The Exposition has drawn all manner of simpleton, charlatan, and huckster. Hyenas come to the lion's den. Such baseless creatures must be culled and reminded of their place.

—from the diary of HH Holmes

IN A CHARACTERISTIC display of congeniality Dr. H.H. Holmes acquiesced to the wishes of his dearest paramour, Ms. Georgiana Yoke, for a day of exploration and frivolity in the nascent fairgrounds sprouting up near his apothecary in Jackson Park. All manner of peddlers showcased their wares while wide-ranging acts vied for the custom of the folks wandering the grounds.

Ms. Yoke's hand rests lightly in the crook of her gentleman caller's arm as they stride with an air of purpose and privilege that marks them as a couple of means as clearly and assuredly as their fine clothes and expensive shoes. If she were being honest with herself, a habit she was not familiar with, she'd have admitted that the thrill and danger of the throng drew her in more strongly than the performances she'd claimed to want to see.

A cold lake wind blew in from the east carrying the coal-laden air deeper into the city. As a result, the omnipresent cloud of smoke and reek of the masses was delightfully absent, and despite Georgiana's secret desires the stroll was uneventful. The aura of malevolence her companion exuded, of which she was blissfully unaware, marked him as a predator of the highest order. The scavengers and opportunistic thieves of the grounds intuitively recognized him for what he truly was, focusing instead on easier prey.

Their explorations carried them past countless peddlers and hawkers. Each staked claim to a small patch of the sandy, marshy land making every effort to draw attention to themselves. Georgiana led the couple through the throngs, glancing at the wares, and marveling at her own worldliness and bravery in exploring the den of hucksters and shopping their goods.

Holmes' professional interest piqued at the sight of a stall, sturdier and more well-built than the others. An elaborate display of 'Foley's Pain Relief' elixir drew his attention from his companion, and as a result she grew restless.

"Dr. Holmes. Your shop is filled with elixirs and tonics of all varieties. I cannot fathom that you will find anything on par with your own wares."

"Quite right," he responded without taking his gaze from the label of the brown bottle he'd picked up. Foley's Pain Relief tonic guaranteed to not only provide analgesia for all manner of injuries, headaches, and neuralgias but to also be effective for colic, diarrhea, and similar bowel complaints.

Handing the merchant a quarter and pocketing the bottle Holmes turned his intense blue eyes to Georgiana. Her pulse quickened, as it always did from his undivided attention.

"Darling, Foley's putting on airs and I need to be abreast of his shenanigans. My patients rely on my expertise to avoid such tom foolery and quackery."

At the mention of his patients, a steady stream of women who fluttered under his piercing blue eyes and attentive ministrations, Georgiana frowned ever so slightly as she was led to further into the exposition grounds.

"Come one, come all! Avail yourselves of this once in a lifetime opportunity to be dazzled and astounded by the strongest woman to have ever lived! A native of the deepest reaches of Amazonia, Diana has the strength of ten men! The fortitude of a bull! And the beauty of a goddess! Such an opportunity will not come again. For the pittance of a nickel you can have a story to tell your children and their children!"

The barker's rich tenor drew the young couple to the tent.

"My good man and madam are you here to lay witness to the most powerful woman in Chicago?"

The man made no effort to hide the appraising gaze of Georgiana or his hungry approval at her countenance.

"A feat of dubious distinction and worth."

Holmes' gaze had settled onto the man, momentarily silencing his retort. He recovered soon, Holmes' slight frame and delicate features bolstering his confidence, who then resumed the well-worn pitch.

"Fine sir, for the pittance of a dime you and your comely friend may see for yourselves Diana's prodigious brawn." After a moment's pause, he continued, "We've two seats on the front row set aside for exceptional patrons, such as yourself."

Georgiana gives her beau's arm an affectionate squeeze as he pays the man for their admission, and they are led to a pair of open seats in the front row for the show that is about to start.

The tent fills to overflowing as Holmes, Georgiana, and other spectators settle into their seats. The row closest to the stage consists of a dozen chairs with cushions, the stained, worn upholstery hidden by the dim lighting. The following two rows are occupied by folks of less robust economic means, crowded and crushed, seated on benches. Unwashed bodies, cigar smoke, and cheap whiskey merge into a miasma that nauseates Holmes, while having a decidedly different effect on his companion.

"Dearest isn't this exhilarating!?"

Holmes' curt nod speaks volumes, and the woman settles in next to him as the barker closes the curtained entrance and walks to the stage upon which is a pair of iron cannonballs connected by a thick shaft, a cluster of iron rods, and most curiously an elongated table-like contraption. Noting the capacity crowd with a look of satisfaction, the barker strode confidently to the front with pockets bulging from the collected nickels.

"My good sirs and madams. Prepare yourself for an astounding view of athletic perfection. My words and eloquence cannot justly describe her skills. Her strength. Her raw power. We are privileged . . . nay honored to bear witness to Diana, Empress of Might!"

The collective gasp of shock at Diana's attire, little more than a length of strategically wrapped white linen offering less modesty than the most scandalous bathing gown, replaced the din of scattered conversation. Diana's purposeful strides highlighted the lines of hard muscle on her thighs and calves.

"Oh my. I bet she could teach those ruffians working at the hotel a thing a two."

A glance at her paramour's disquieting expression dismissed thoughts of conversation. Georgiana took her hand from the crook of his arm, folded them, and placed them in her lap. She'd seen that look before, and it troubled her.

Diana's impressive displays of strength amazed the crowd. Weights were lifted overhead, iron rods twisted into decorations, and a gaggle volunteers from the crowd climbed onto the table-like device which she placed securely on her back, and with a grunt of effort lifted it clear from the floor. Throughout the demonstrations of strength Diana's poise never wavered, her smile did not falter, despite the gritted teeth behind it and the thin sheen of perspiration.

The crowd's enthusiastic cheers and cries of astonishment buoyed her to greater displays of strength, and yet one man was notably unimpressed from his front row seat.

"My good sir! Is your own vigor not bolstered by Diana's remarkable athleticism?"

The promoter addressed the crowd next in mock stage whisper, "Or intimidated?"

Georgiana stiffened involuntarily as the crowd guffawed at the addendum.

"Sir, I jest and apologize sincerely for my absence of manners. I'm quite sure your lack of enjoyment is the result of poor digestion, or other malady. May I suggest a draught of Foley's?"

The crowd's attention shifted to Holmes who maintained the perfect stillness of a tightly coiled spring. His face reddened, and knuckles turned white. Oblivious to the danger he was placing himself in the showman continued his jeers.

"Before you are a pair of ordinary iron slugs conjoined by blacksmith with a handle for easy grasping. If you are able to lift it a handspan you'll earn a sawbuck and the admiration of the crowd."

Through gritted teeth Holmes replied, "I do not need your money, nor the admiration of the scalawags in this abominable tent."

"Ahh, so you demure. Very well. Perhaps your comely companion?"

Holmes stood as if to leave, placed a hand on Ms. Yoke to remain seated, and ascended the steps to the stage. Composure regained he shook hands with his antagonist, and set himself to task.

A web of veins stood in relief on Holmes' forehead, pulsating in time with his efforts, but alas he could not lift the iron weight. It lay firmly stuck to stage, immoveable. Strength exhausted he looked in consternation at the iron pig so firmly bound by gravity's forces.

Diana watched the display in bored silence from the side of the stage. The events have played out countless times before, and no one else had yet been able to lift the dumbbell, it's excessively thickened handle requiring a grip strength that virtually none possess. None but her. Her practiced lift was greeted with the roar of the crowd, and flattened affect of her competition. His face could have been carved from quarried marble, and then the mask broke. He smiled at her, for her, and walked from the stage with the poise and composure of a gentleman.

Holmes escorted Georgiana to her home in silence. Neither spoke of the contest, and soon she was left at her door with the bottle of Foley's and the insinuation that she might do well with a hefty dose tonight before bed.

The note from Dr. Holmes requesting a private show wasn't the first such missive that Diana had received; truth be told she had one almost every day and they represented a substantial portion of her income. As was her usual Diana left to meet her benefactor without an escort, once less person to share her earnings with and she never found a need for a bodyguard or other nonsense.

The address, in nearby Englewood, led her to an enormous building and the barbershop it housed. At this time of night it wasn't unusual for a shop to be empty, and she had been summoned so the unlocked door didn't concern her either. The room was softly lit by a kerosene lamp, further proof that she was expected, and a quick glance confirmed its lack of inhabitants. The wall length bench for waiting patrons was empty, as were the three barber's chair. Choosing a chair over the hard bench she set herself to wait for the tardy Dr. Holmes.

The man stalking Diana had been warned by Holmes of her strength, athleticism, and that he believed her to be a gentleman masquerading as a woman. Pitezel knew that a weighted cosh could fell the strongest person, and he'd damned if he was going to risk losing this one. Holmes was in a right fit tonight and crossing him would mean more than a loss of a paycheck. He'd heard her footfalls on the wooden floor, and the telltale squeaking of a barber's chair slowly rotating told him her exact location.

Pitezel intoned a silent thanks for his good fortune and crept from the door behind the chairs. He wasted no time, gave no quarter, and unleashed upon her the unfettered violence of the deranged. Diana slumped forward, fell from her perch, and lay bleeding from the blunt force trauma. Pitezel broke into an icy sweat as he thought he'd kill his master's prize, only calming when he noted the rhythmic rise and fall of respiration.

Grunting and cursing Pitezel carried Diana's bruised, bleeding, and unconscious body up to the third floor where she was unceremoniously deposited into the dungeon via the chute purpose built for such tasks. Diana would wait there for Holmes, who had other plans for the evening.

Mortimer McDowell's choice in profession was a disappointment to his mother, but one that he embraced. Lazy and with a quick wit, he was ideally suited to the life of a traveling entertainer. As was his habit after the final show Mortimer made himself scarce when the time to clean up came around. Hidden in the shadows, far from crowds he enjoyed a bowl of tobacco. The pipe was an affectation of course, but one the shabby man enjoyed.

Clinging to the eve above with preternatural strength Holmes observed his prey. This common man's tortuous death would slake the pangs of raging malevolence within him and perhaps provide insight into the work yet to come. He would take his time, expend his frustration, and save the woman as an offering to his mistress.

Holmes dropped silently from above, landing with nary a sound, grappling his prey as securely as if he had an extra pair of arms, and rendering him insensate with chloroform in moments. Unlike McDowell, Holmes was a man of precision. The chloroform's soporific effects waned in perfect attunement with the powerful paralysis induced by the curare Holmes had dosed him with. Mortimer was perfectly awake, aware, and sensate, yet the paralytic bound him more effectively than any camisole.

McDowell's inability to affect muscular movement prevented him from seeing his surroundings, a problem that Holmes resolved with a pair of exacting cuts from the French finger knife he preferred for delicate work. It was then that McDowell realized the depths of hell to which he had fallen. The blepharectomy was soon followed by a partial enucleation. Nothing could prepare McDowell's mind for the twisted perspective from his eye, its attachment to the optic nerve intact, resting on his cheek. Casually Holmes snipped the nerve, and with it McDowell's sanity.

Holmes worked in absolute silence, lost in thought reliving his lengthy discussions with Chappell on the practical art of articulation. He hypothesized that with the right techniques and processes the post-humous wiring, a lengthy and tedious process, could be eliminated.

The key, he believed, was for the ligament's blood supply to be maintained while the subject was undergoing treatment with the preservative solution that imbued the connections with the strength and elasticity they would require for use in perpetuity by the medical schools Holmes sold them to.

The vivisection of Mortimer McDowell continued through the night into the wee hours of the morning. Holmes took in his handywork with a tight smile. His patient's skin lay draped on a drying rack, next to it a bucket of glistening, red muscles, and finally a tray on the work bench with the organs known to be unnecessary for the prolongation of life. What remained was a nightmarish mass of meat, offal, and skeletal extremities. Countless forceps protruded from the neck, axilla, and groin staying the unnecessary loss of blood.

Mortimer's gibbering, fractured mind retained enough lucidity to welcome the release of drowning as it was immersed in the waiting tank of preservative.

Shageriin Raider

A successful harvest depends on the farmer spending countless hours in the dirt sowing and tending the fields for weeks, months, even years. The hunter studies, understands, and stalk their prey following scat and trails through the darkest jungles with preternatural patience akin to the lions of the savannah. And there is the arachnid. The perfect, silent, efficient hunter. Waiting for a foolish morsel. The choicest victual to drop in their lap, no need to fatten or flatter before the slaughter, merely a razor's cut, a reaping, and a final exhalation of breath.

—From the diary of HH Holmes

Adventure.

THAT WAS THe first word that popped into Shageriin's mind when he finally arrived in Chicago. He had traveled the world, explored places barely known to man, and collected artifacts so fine he would surely please the gods. When he left Nanjing the first time, it really had been an adventure. The rebellion left his city and his people broken, but his sister was married to a kind man, and Shageriin felt no guilt in escaping the country to explore new places. When his sister's husband died in the rebellion, the thought of adventure transformed into the goal of mere survival.

But his nomad spirit sent restlessness through his blood. He left once again, this time for the World's Columbian Exposition in the strange land of America. It was not his first experience at a World's Fair—just last year he walked the warm streets of Madrid, and a few years before that, Paris. Shageriin doubted any fair could outdo Paris, with the newly constructed Eiffel Tower as the archway into the plaza, the graceful curves of its architecture were an impressive feat.

Architecture, however, was not why Shageriin came to Chicago. The fair meant crowds where people of all walks of life mingled, people from around the world who had surely paid well to get here. There would be buyers. Collectors. People who knew of powers hidden within the artifacts Shageriin gathered.

The World's Columbian Exposition welcomed all into its white marble clutches, or so it claimed. Signs promised exhibits of rare art, dancers, cuisine from around the globe, but the posters tacked up that encouraged visitors to see "exotic people" on display sent nausea roiling through his gut. He had been at the mercy of men who viewed other people as commodities, as tokens to be bartered for money. Never again.

Shageriin knew he contained power. His parents died trying to protect the knowledge of his power. He could understand languages he'd never spoken, find artifacts others had died for, and felt there was more untapped within him, buried deep beneath the fear of his own possibilities.

He shook the dwelling thoughts away and walked deeper into the White City. Despite his earlier hesitation, he couldn't help but think the view was one of the most extraordinary sights he'd come across, and his eyes had witnessed much. He had stumbled upon great and grand beauty around the Earth—sights in nature that rendered him breathless, waterfalls and temples as picturesque as paintings, but there was something about this great fair, this impossible thing in the middle of a soot-stained city creating a rare splendor all its own.

The architecture was indeed stunning, pure marble erected into huge buildings as far as he could see. Neo-Classical buildings surrounded a great basin, and the huge Ferris Wheel he heard whispers of seemed to loom over all. Electric incubators attracted a flock of people who rushed past Shageriin, and he stood behind them and marveled over the lightbulbs.

The sidewalks curved around the waterways like a seascape town rather than the midst of a city. Replicas of Viking ships and even a Japanese dragon boat rocked gently in the waves. The scent of spice and meats wafted into the air from nearby exhibits of German and

Irish villages. Shageriin's stomach grumbled in response, but he kept onward. Everything wildly overstimulated his senses.

The White City blinded him, and he scoffed at its plain color; what purity did these people think they were entitled to, anyway? He had only been in America once before, briefly near the western shore. He preferred the coast with its crashing waves and sea-foam scent to crowds of people.

Shageriin was not afraid of new places, but here, in the middle of all this white marble, something darker lurked. A shadow he sensed but could not find. Not yet.

He tightened the leather satchel on his back and walked toward a recreation of a French village where a pretty woman was selling food.

"A croissant please," he said to her; the lure of something flaky and buttery became too much for him to pass up.

She smiled and took his coins, and then handed him the pastry. "Thank you kindly."

"What's your name?" She beamed at him with a bright smile, and he thought of the lightbulb everyone in the street had stopped to peer at. The sun caught her raven hair, and Shageriin could have sworn tones of blue resided in such midnight strands.

"Sean Baider," he replied, an alias he used before, especially around Americans.

The woman started to say something, but a deeper voice cut her off.

"Sean?"

Shageriin spun around to find a familiar face staring at him. The man was about his own height, but better dressed. Shageriin knew the strength that hid beneath the silk clothes, too.

"Excuse me," he said to the French woman. "And thank you again."

She smiled sadly as the men turned to leave, and a chill planted itself in Shageriin's spine. Shade from the great tree above the spot where the man led him blocked out the sun. The bumbling crowd faded to a murmur as they blended themselves in with the shadows.

"Sean? This is the name you answer to now?" the man scoffed.

Shageriin shrugged. "These Americans, they can only pronounce so much."

Together they grinned beneath the great tree with its spring blossoms and laughed.

"What are you doing here, Li Yu?" Shageriin bit into his croissant and savored each warm mouthful. "I thought the Great Qing forbade anyone from taking part in the Americans desire to have a Chinese exhibition?"

"They did, but then the dynasty grew jealous and wanted to know what was happening. I am here to report on what I find, officially."

"And unofficially?"

Li ushered Shageriin away from the thickest parts of the crowd. "Unofficially, I heard a deserter might appear hear to sell a rare artifact he had found on his adventures, and I thought, hm, I know just the fool who that must be."

Shageriin laughed again, but could not shake the sensation of being carefully watched, of being tracked by something just out of his eyesight.

They walked along, and the shadows followed. "There is a restless spirit here."

"A growing darkness. I sensed it, too." Li glanced behind them but kept moving. "There is darkness within the empire, too, but it is different than this darkness. Yet you ran away. Ran from one shadow to another."

"I saw an opportunity," Shageriin explained. "This power we have been gifted, to understand things others cannot, I can use it to help my sister."

"The empire needs men like us to protect it. To protect your sister. We cannot do that abroad."

"We are hardly men."

"That's the point," Li whispered. "Our powers, we could do so much more."

"And then what, be bound to an empire on the verge of collapse?"

Li huffed and crossed his arms. "We are on the brink of war— and then after that will come collapse. Come home. You have ancient power inside you, if you are only willing to use it."

Shageriin shook his head and tightened the straps of his leather satchel.

"Fine. Collect your trinkets and get your money."

Anger surged through Shageriin, molten and untamed. "Do you

know what happens to widows, Li? They have not been treated kindly under this dynasty. Do you know how many have been driven to take their own life away? If that happens to my sister, I will never forgive myself. I will get my money, and my trinkets, and I will free her."

Li sighed and exhaustion crept into the wrinkles around his eyes. "You have been away too long. Come with me."

Li led Shageriin out of the White City and into the connecting Midway Plaisance. Here, Shageriin found familiar faces. The Chinese and Japanese exhibits were housed in Midway rather than between the white marble—housed away from civilization.

He watched the Chinese Chicagoans and the familiar nausea crept up his throat at the way people could be used like living items in a museum for the entertainment of others.

"Why did you take me here?"

"There are others with power. Dark power tinged in blood. People are searching for their identity all around you, Shageriin. Not just suicidal widows."

Rage bloomed anew as he turned away from Li. "Why don't you go back to your opium dens? That's all you ever wanted anyway. Don't think I have forgotten."

Shageriin turned and marched back down the street. Evening had come upon them fast, and the setting sun cast sherbet tones across the horizon. The sweet scents of delicious food faded and mixed with coal and manure the further he walked away from the fair. A tug on his satchel caused him to stumble back.

A drunk man peered at the bag and then at Shageriin. Stubble lined the man's thin, pale face. "Interesting things in there, boy."

"Unless you're paying, they have no interest in you."

Li Yu strode over and more irritation flooded through Shageriin, but he kept his mouth shut, figuring Li would have his back if this man wanted to take anything by force.

The same bone-gripping chill he'd felt earlier drowned his body. As if he'd swallowed cold shadows.

An earth-shattering scream tore all three men away from their staring contest. The White City was just in view, but a crowd had gathered around the base of a tall building, and more shrieking emitted into the darkening skies. Shageriin raced over with Li, but the drunk man stayed in the alley.

Shageriin peered into the crowd where rivulets of crimson stained the sidewalk. A rush of voices from the crowd talked over each other.

"He just fell."

"Oh my God. From the roof?"

"Is he dead? He must be dead."

"Get the children away."

A woman fainted and her husband caught her, hauling her limp body away. Shageriin moved forward and saw the man, a worker, on the ground. His head had split open the way Shageriin imagined a watermelon would if you dropped it from a very high building. Scarlet stained the White City as the sun continued to disappear, casting darkness around the hysteric crowd. A doctor came, but it was of course too late. No one could have survived that. Bloody footprints from people who had stepped in the man's brain matter left streaks across the clean sidewalks, painting the scene in red violence.

"Come on," Li grabbed Shageriin by the arm and hauled him away.

He could barely move. When he closed his eyes, he saw his sister. Is that what she would do if she were left alone and penniless? If no one could help her before the collapse of the very empire . . .

Shageriin freed himself from Li's grip and trudged back to the drunk man in the alley.

"You, what do you want? Do you have money?"

The man laughed and took a swig from a bottle he had stored beneath his ratty coat.

"Nah, but my boss does. He'd be interested in anything, let's say, out of the ordinary."

"Where can I find him?"

"Head down to Englewood and look for the castle, that monstrosity of a building." The man cackled. "Ask for Mr. Holmes." He stumbled away before Shageriin could ask anything else.

He turned toward Li. "Do you know the building?"

"You can't miss it. The architecture of a barbarian, that thing is. He must be rich."

The echoes of people still horrified by the fallen man reverberated around them, and Shageriin was anxious to escape it all. Blood and shadows. The sun was nearly gone, taking all light and warmth with its slumber.

"Will you walk with me to this place?"

Li hesitated. "When I smoke, a darkness comes to form around the edges of the haze. There are shadows scurrying here, and there is darkness beneath all this foolish, white marble. But the darkness I see down that road, my friend. It is a darkness I will not walk. You do not need to walk it either."

"I have walked in shadows before."

"The great power within you that you bury, that you fear. Use it now."

Li Yu placed a hand on Shageriin's shoulder and then walked away. Dim blackness consumed all except for flickering streetlamps and the blinking lights of the fair now far in the background. The White City faded into the gloom, and suddenly all that impressive marble meant nothing, no matter how many new inventions for light they tried to use to make it glow.

The building was indeed monstrous. Shageriin couldn't tell if it was meant to be composed of shops, a hotel, or some combination of different things. Windows of different sizes shed blurred light through the glass and out onto the street.

Shageriin entered what appeared to be an open jewelry store since the rest of the bottom shops were dark.

"Hello?" he called out into the stillness. A faint light glowed behind the counter, the proprietor's office, perhaps.

"I'm sorry," a man's voice called. "We only have room for female tenants tonight. You can try the Franklin's place down the road."

Shageriin stepped closer to the counter but kept himself within arm's reach of the door. "No, I have something . . . an associate, I think, of yours, mentioned you might be interested in purchasing a rare item I have." His heart raced and he could hear the stutter in his own words. The ice of the shadow's grip that had been following him extended even more here, in this dusty shop. "He was drunk."

Get out, a voice whispered inside Shageriin's head. He apologized for disturbing the man hidden in the office and bolted toward the door, but the dim light flickered off and something clicked in the darkness. The door?

"What is the item?" The man's voice was right beside Shageriin now, cold breath down his neck like icy feathers.

"A dagger. From ruins more ancient than I have ever discovered before."

Li Yu had told Shageriin to tap into his powers, and he tried, but the evil of this place, of this man, drowned out all the light. Shageriin's blood-fire combatted with freezing shadows, but the darkness won. His very bones were frozen, on the verge of being shattered and forcing his body to collapse.

A sharp rip sliced through his leather satchel as the other man, the creature, took the bag. Shageriin leapt for it, feeling his way through the blackness to try and get the dagger first—hoping it might offer some protection.

He tried to scream, but a sick gurgling emerged from the cavern of his mouth instead. In perfect silence, the other man forced the dagger across Shageriin's throat, and in this strange moment that came before the blood spilled forth, he closed his eyes and sent a prayer to his sister, hoping it would be much longer before she chose to join him in the afterlife . . . or perhaps she was already there. Waiting with a split watermelon that resembled a man's head, waiting somewhere where shadows morph into crimson and spill down on the white marble erected by men who have built murderous castles.

H.H. Holmes

In perusing my prior notes, I can see that the instincts and impulses leading to their ensnarement were most fortuitous. Each pulled forth, draw into my home by an irresistibly subtle force. My lady's delicate manipulations most efficacious with sublime beauty. An ode to her countenance given form and function. Enshrouded and bound as they are the time draws near for my apotheosis. The formulae and rituals have worked exquisitely. Despite their injuries, affronts, and considerable time it took to gather they await at the ready.

She too weaves her machinations. Her touch is already apparent at the Exposition. I alone see through the veil. See the world for what it truly is. For now . . .

—From the diary of HH Holmes

THE THING WITH death is that people mistook its dark clutch as something permanent. Dr. Holmes knew better.

The precision at which Dr. Holmes, nee Mr. Mudgett, arranged the tools of his trade belied the excitement that fired within his gut. His prey was captured, the landscape's transformation had begun, and the building anticipation of his own transformation welled within, exciting him physically, emotionally, and spiritually.

PAUL

PAUL'S INERT BODY was laid out on the examining table before Holmes. He was one of five, each arranged with the precision attributed to apothecaries and physicians. Holmes would have a busy and exhilarating night tonight. He found himself looking forward to the total exhaustion and feeling of spent purpose that came afterwards almost as much as the acts themselves. Those moments of torpid recovery and blessed oblivion were their own sweet release.

"A veritable handful of prey," Holmes said to himself with a tight smile as he broke the tomb-like silence of his basement surgery theater and began his examinations.

Each subject was held in the literal moment of their final exhalation and penultimate heartbeat. The next breath and heartbeat had not been missed, and so they remained in a twilight of sorts. The opportunity to assuage his needs on subjects that were both living and dead was a gift he prized above all others.

Holmes' fascination had not been diminished by the recent events to which Paul had been subjected. This was Holmes' first opportunity to lay hands on the worker, and he relished the intimacy.

Holmes stood before his prey, closed his eyes, and took into himself a prodigious inhalation through his nostrils which he held within. The air brought with it myriad scents that his knacks, bequeathed by his mistress, transformed into an encyclopedic understanding of his prey.

Through the stench of burnt hair, he smelled the blood that told him of Paul's decision to choose a different path than the one that Mother Nature laid out for him. He noted that the blood held the muted aroma of the anemic. Unsurprising for someone so malnourished. The fetid stench of Paul's final bowel movement confirmed this suspicion, not that Holmes doubted himself.

At the apex of his breath, his eyes opened in surprise when he discovered the odorous cancer that had begun to eat away at Paul's lungs, and the tantalizingly sweet scents of Mavis and Taavi. Cracker Jack be damned, there is no confection as alluring as a child at play.

"I do so love the sounds of children."

When he released the breath, Holmes set to work on Paul. He began by cleaning the body. A process made more challenging by the manner of his tortuous captivity. Sheets of burnt skin were removed with the marks of ash and blood. Paul's clothing had afforded a modicum of protection to the bulk of his body, leaving only his hands and head exposed.

The tobacco stains and callouses that marked Paul as a laborer were no more. They'd been removed with his skin. His hair, already short, had been consumed by the conflagration. Paul's cartilaginous features—lips, nose, and ears—were salvageable, as were his eyelids.

Holmes was thankful for the last. He'd not yet honed his skills sufficiently to rebuild eyelids. Holmes allowed himself a moment of quiet reflection on his experiments on the barker before returning to the job at hand.

Holmes' mental checklist included replacing lost skin, consumed hair, and excising the cancerous lungs within his subject. The last thrilled him physically and intellectually as he thought of what he'd replace the diseased respiratory organs with.

The hair was easy enough. He'd learned to work with silk a decade ago as a neophyte under the tutelage of masters of the craft. From the vast supply he kept on hand he chose a lustrous auburn. Paul's hair had been a wholly forgettable brown before, and Holmes thought himself magnanimous in bequeathing the improvement.

The tedium of implanting countless strands of spider's silk did not suit Holmes' temperament. He found his gaze drawn again and again to Paul's torso, and the prize it held. A sadist through and through he found the masochistic delay intriguing and challenged himself to not give into the urge.

Pronouncing the deed done, Holmes stepped away, opened a nearby cabinet, and chose from dozens of spools of flayed skin. The color was a near perfect match, and in his rush, he decided it would suit just fine. Hands were gloved, the skull masked, and Holmes' stirrings of obsession returned with a vengeance, a sure sign of a job well done.

Holmes eschewed breaks during his ministrations as a sign of weak constitution and insufficient will. He moved from task to task with purposeful confidence assured in his abilities. The answer to the final riddle, how best to replace Paul's failing lungs, came to him in a flash of divine inspiration.

Holmes held firmly his preferred French finger and began with a crossbody incision at the lowest point of the pectoral muscles. A series of tissue retractors held the skin and muscle at bay as he excised the blackened, tarry lungs. They were deposited into a waiting receptacle of organs and offal for later disposal in the slaughter yards, or perhaps as offering to Lake Michigan.

To fill the gaping hole in Paul's torso, Holmes left his post at the examination table. When he returned, he held a dripping sheaf of organic pages bound by a hollow tube of white cartilage. The organ resembled nothing so much as an opened book with feathery, glistening pages. The book's "spine" attached to his subject's trachea, and the pages fanned out within the thorax.

Excitement flooded Holmes as he made the required connections, removed the retractors, and sewed the skin together. He took a step back in marvel at his genius and the improvements he made on the flawed creature he'd known as Paul. Flush with success, he moved to the next table.

Paul's heart beat once and went silent again.

DIANA

HOLMES' ENERGY SELDOM left him; his basement laboratory was a timeless place. Within its walls he felt neither hunger, nor thirst, nor fatigue. His attentive ministrations invigorated him, fueled his labors to new heights of appalling invention. He suspected eldritch forces at work, but never questioned them or the unexpected changes She sometimes made to the castle. He thanked Her for the subtle guidance, and continued on his way.

Before him lay the woman from the vaudeville show. The gas he'd piped into her chamber while she waited had done its job, and without a single blemish to mar her physicality that he found so enticing. A rare specimen indeed. Holmes excitement grew to a crescendo when he noted that she'd worn her show costume under her street attire as requested in his missive.

Holmes stood over Diana's body and began his examination with a visual inspection. Enveloped in the serenity of his surgery, he noted that she was without a doubt a woman, and an extraordinary one at that. The exquisitely developed musculature of her calves, thighs, arms, and shoulders reminded him of the lithe, purposeful strength of a swimmer or acrobat. Her features spoke of Portuguese and South American ancestry. It seemed the barker had not been lying when he claimed Amazonian heritage for her. She was the physical superior to Pitezel, Chappell, or any of the men working at on the hotel.

Next, he shifted his attention to her hands and forearms. The tools by which she, and that hated showman, had humiliated him. Thick, rough calluses coated the pads of her palms and interior of each finger. The fingers were thickened as if by growth of the minute muscles that lined them. Her corded forearms would have been at home on any of the bricklayers he'd known. Holmes noted of her scarred knuckles. Pitezel had similar marks.

"What path led you to me?"

The physical examination followed the visual one. Holmes' delicate fingers prodded and kneaded the woman's tissues to learn more of her. This process was unnecessary from a scientific perspective. An observer to his repeated violation would note the rapturous job which played across Holmes' visage and know the true reason for the intimacy. For all the airs he put on about scientific curiosity, expanding his knowledge, and uncovering secrets Holmes was a petty sadist. He simply enjoyed inflicting pain and humiliation.

Holmes washed his hands and face in the nearby basin after. The ritualistic cleansing cleared the heady afterglow of his ministrations, and brought his thoughts back to Diana. He had no techniques to improve her bodily strength beyond its prodigious levels; her constitution had been robust and organs healthy.

"Those damnable hands."

In a flash of inspiration, Holmes' thoughts turned to the future when he'd need allies whose weapons could hide in plain sight. Strangulations and beatings would be seen as rewards his followers would appreciate. Strong hands such as hers would be invaluable to them. Further study was warranted, and improvements developed.

Degloving the hands, which he'd marveled at, was the first step. There was no need for delicacy, Holmes' excitement had returned, and he set himself to task with fevered joy. A bistoury sliced through the layers of skin just above her wrist, and with its blunt probe he teased it from the muscles beneath. A firm pull with forceps and the muscles lay revealed.

With the hand so exposed, the probe separated the tendons of each finger from their muscular surroundings. Again, the basement's queer properties took hold on Holmes, and time stood still for the tedious work of teasing the stringy connections free.

Each hand was dipped for precisely eight seconds into a waiting bowl of carbolic acid. Cleansing the muscles and enhancing the permeability of the sinews was vital to the success of the experiment. They bubbled still from their treatments when Diana's mutilated hands were assuaged in an unctuous solution of Holmes' invention based on the writings of the sacred Book of Eibon.

If his interpretation of the texts was accurate the suspension would imbue the tendons, ligaments, and muscles with the hardness of marble while they kept their supple dexterity. The process would take days, possibly weeks. Holmes never concerned himself with failure or delays. There were always other victims, and he had all the time in the world.

SHAGERIIN

THE MAN'S THROAT had waterfalled open like juiced cherries. Judging by the large satchel and array of eccentric objects within, he was a traveler. A little younger than Holmes and of Asian descent, adventurous enough to come to the fair, to step within the spider's web and not care about the possibility of being ensnared.

The hunt for artifacts, Holmes wondered as he turned the bizarre dagger over in his scarlet-stained hands, was it as satisfying as a kill? Did crawling through crumbling tombs and cutting down vines only to find some rare, glistening treasure elicit the same excitement as watching the light leave someone's lifeless eyes?

The dagger contained strange powers within the intricate swirls designed on the blade. A small skull rested on the top with two ruby eyes in its sockets. Such alchemy was not for him to understand; he had his own abilities. Setting aside the blade, Holmes rustled through the man's bag and discovered a few papers of identification. *Shageriin Baider.*

"Mr. Baider," Holmes said softly to the isolated chamber as he circled the body restrained on the metal table. "Thank you for your cooperation."

He hummed a slow tune as he worked, and a large kiln on the opposite side of the room crackled a fire song in rhythm with the doctor's melody. All else was quiet down here between asbestos-lined walls and thick padding to keep the space soundproof. Doors were locked and secret chutes had been secured; no patrons resided in the hotel rooms, and he ensured all workers were sent home for the night.

Throats were so delicate, repairing a broken one demanded intense concentration. The art of resurrection, much like with the near opposite task of articulation, was something one must be willing to work patiently at. But truly, anyone could learn to articulate a body, to tenderly strip its flesh like peeling delicate petals from a meaty flower. To restore life, however, was a power instilled in Holmes since birth, but he spent much time learning and nurturing his abilities over the years.

The vocal cords would not mend perfectly—they were too much like shredded wires, impossible to fix the exact way they once rested within a body.

Being the creature that he was, Holmes contained resources to amend his hasty murder of the man. From within his own abdomen, he reached deep inside a hidden spinneret gland nestled behind overlapping folds of flesh. He withdrew tendrils of fine silk for trapping prey, but instead used it to wrap around the jaggedly slashed throat of the traveler.

Steely cobwebs spun around muscle tissue, mending the windpipe, absorbing the scent of copper in the air, and slowly healing the traumatic force Holmes had inflicted upon the larynx. He continued to hum, to chant . . . to instill a sense of vivacity within the soul he'd taken. The corpse bloomed into new life, and cadaver morphed back into man. Shageriin Baider lived once more. For now.

Restlessness filled Shageriin from his first waking moment, and he tossed about the table with his eyes closed. A name bubbled from his lips and his brow narrowed in worry.

"What were you dreaming?" Holmes whispered.

The man mumbled but did not open his eyes. "My sister . . . "

"Your sister is dead," Holmes stated. He had no idea, of course, about any state this sister might be in, but it seemed like a good way to wake the man up and bring him back into the real world.

Shageriin bolted up, alert. His dark eyes opened wide and he flailed so hard he broke through the fabric wrist restraints. Holmes stepped out of the way as the man madly paced around the basement, making bewildered noises and coughing as if something were caught in his throat.

"What did you do?" Shageriin spit out the words, like a hacking cat.

"I fixed you," Holmes replied simply.

Shageriin stopped and caught his distorted reflection from the shine of the kiln. He tried to glance at his throat, but Holmes doubted he could see the art in the cobweb stitches like he did.

"Enough of this. You will rest until the others are ready." Holmes loomed over Shageriin.

Venom brewed high up in Holmes mouth, stored away in what would be the small fangs of spiders, but for him resided deep within his gums. He grabbed Shageriin's face firmly and spit venom into the other man's face. The glue-like substance connected the traveler's head to the wall, keeping him fixed there long enough for Holmes to finish with the rest of the cadavers in the basement.

VICTOR

THE ARCHITECT'S BODY remained on the concrete where it'd fallen after the acid bath. The caustic solution ate away at his bones and teeth quite fervently, but it took an entire day. Holmes bent down to adjust the man's position so that he could perform his work on the floor. The acerbic stench of burned away flesh hit his nostrils immediately, but he breathed it in deep.

The cranium and neck were completely devoid of any epidermis. He reached forward to gently straighten the man out, but the skull's remaining structure crumbled like dry shortbread. Holmes cursed. He knew from the start he'd have to build the man a new skull, but he hoped at least some structure might remain for him to work with. No matter.

As he had used webbing to mend Shageriin's throat, he could use a stickier silk to help frame a new skull for the architect, but he would still need bones.

"Mr. Emory," he addressed the corpse. "I hope you will appreciate this." The doctor gracefully navigated his way across the extensive basement to gather materials.

Her cranium was thicker than Victor's, but less wide. It wouldn't look quite right, not like his original bones, but a skull was a skull. Nothing else remained of Lorelei Emory. After he'd finished stripping her skeleton of flesh and organs, he had cleaned the bones and sold them to a respectable college, sans the skull.

"Call it a 'memento mori' eh?" Holmes chuckled as he went to work, first drawing the adhesive material out of his body to craft a kind of stencil to work with. The webs merged together and twisted their sticky, white sinews to form a blueprint. From there, Holmes crafted a sunken neck made entirely of cobweb, and then wedged the bones onto Victor like a sick puzzle.

Creating new eyes for the man was not an impossible task, but Holmes opted to instead wrap a cloth around the empty eye sockets. He infused scarlet whispers into the new head, and the man of mostly flesh and partially bone awakened to the world of the living.

"I am sorry about the darkness," Holmes said. "I wish you could see what I have created for you. The architecture of a face, who but you could appreciate the way these bones fit together?"

The man shivered as he sat up from the ground. He braced his hands against the concrete and then raised one to touch his bony face.

"She lives on within you, for now."

Victor shivered. "Lorelei? I can hear you in my head. Where are you?"

Holmes smiled, not expecting this surprise. Memento mori indeed . . .

"Well," he thought about the different kinds of powers in the world, all he'd learned about, yet there were so many more. "Memories live on sometimes, in extraordinary ways. It seems your Lorelei held a kind of magic in her bones, perhaps. Maybe she will help you when we begin."

"Begin what?"

"The ritual," Holmes said and blinked, as if it were the most obvious thing in the world. "I needed five, and here you all are. So willing. So adventurous. So brave. But ah, do not worry. Lorelei is excluded from this. She was merely an appetizer, let's say."

Victor flung himself at Holmes, but the blinded man was easy to sidestep. He darted around the basement and made quite the scene, this creature in a businessman's suit with web and bone protruding from his collar. He tripped over a table's leg and Holmes dashed forward to catch the man.

"I admire the fight in you, but I'd save that energy for later."

He wrestled the undead architect toward the wall where metal cuffs swayed from their fastenings in the wall, much more reliable than fabric restraints.

"Careful now, let's not shatter poor Lorelei's remains," he said as Victor fought him, but then the former architect calmed. His shaking hands touched his exposed skull once more, and a terrible wail of grief rang out in hallow echoes between bones.

Holmes secured the man's wrists into the cuffs and left him to his mourning.

Almost there. Almost done.

Rosine

THE END WAS at last in sight. Exhaustion crept through Holmes, but the determination to finish this was stronger than his fatigue. The last of the five was of course the fair Ms. Van Tassel. For the most part, she remained unharmed. After she'd fallen down to the darkness of Holmes' devilish chamber, he'd crept through the blackness and chloroformed her into unconsciousness. With the sharp end of a needle, he'd injected her pale skin with poison, and let her die peacefully in twilight sleep.

She had to die for the final ritual to be completed. They all did. Strengthening the connections between this world and the Dreamlands was a task that demanded the twice-dead. Their dual nature, antithetical to natural order, weakened the boundaries. Their sacrifice to the Great Old One would provide the needed anchor.

Though Rosine believed herself to be alone in the dark before she died, the spiders had been there, too. Watching with kaleidoscopic eyes and whispering throughout the castle . . . as they were even now. Their chattering sent electric jolts of anticipation through Holmes, arousing his senses back into sharp alertness as he continued his work.

Rosine's resemblance to Holmes' own paramour, Ms. Yoke, lent an unexpected tenderness throughout his thoughts as he straightened her body on the icy table. While the woman would require no manufacturing of bones or a redesigned throat, she did need new blood for Holmes to bring her back into his world.

Xenotransfusion. Holmes had never attempted it before, but it seemed simple enough. He read the case studies and knew how to perform a traditional blood transfusion, so deriving the blood from an animal instead of a human surely would prove equally effectual in the end. In truth, he could have easily snatched a wandering nomad or homeless youth from the streets of Chicago without stirring suspicion, but the curiosity in his brain sparked madly at the thought of performing something new, something he had not yet experimented with before.

In the case study, less than ten percent of the animal's blood had been used for the transfusion. Pigs were quite common for the process, but he refused to pump the old life of swine into Rosine. A contact at the local slaughterhouse owed Holmes quite the favor for his help in destroying a body Holmes had asked no questions about.

The doctor requested lamb's blood. Quite a substantial amount of it. The irony of using God's chosen motif for his mistress's sacrifice was not lost on Holmes.

He had drained Rosine completely and sent her old blood down a drain installed in the basement's floor. Her body remained suspended in a kind of stasis where, with his power, he could keep parts of her believing they were alive. Her skin, her organs, her very meat sang a soft song to him as he arranged her arm and stuck the IV carefully into a vein. Over a gallon of lamb's blood waited in a bucket beside where Holmes sat upright on a stool.

He stroked tangled hair away from Rosine's face and began the transfusion, keeping the song her body sang afloat in his mind—he even left her ruby necklace fastened around the soft throat. Her good deeds had transferred quite the amount of wealth to him as it were, let her awaken in new blood with something beautiful and familiar on her person to keep her sane.

Hours passed by and Holmes found himself meditating in the quiet arctic of the basement. The others remained silent, still weak from their new bodies, but he knew they'd get strong soon enough. It was time for Rosine to join them.

Holmes went to her and placed his fingertips gently on her temple, listening to the flow of new blood throughout her veins. Darkness lingered like rotten marrow, but he assumed it was due to the complications of bringing a once-dead body back into the living realm. He helped her gradually wake up and watched as long eyelashes fluttered.

Rosine groaned and shook, her body covered in the sheen of sweat as she struggled against the restraints around her ankles. He had left her wrists free to properly execute the transfusion.

Holmes held his hands up as if in surrender. "Ms. Van Tassel, please calm yourself."

The woman growled and Holmes caught a glimpse of blackened gums. She swiped out at him and scratched a ragged cut onto his left hand. He jumped back and examined the superficial wound, noting how quickly it seemed to itch and bloom with red.

Something had been wrong in the lamb's blood. He moved back further and examined Rosine at a distance. She snarled again and her eyes, once bright like gemstones, had dulled to coal.

Of course.

"You're rabid," he declared to the basement and his audience of half-conscious bodies. Either way, it would have to do. Rosine lost her likeness to Ms. Yoke in this unexpected, infected state, but Holmes found the feral glimmer in her eyes enthralling. There was a challenge to be had, not only by him now, but by the other four who would become Ms. Van Tassel's companions as together, they weaved a sacrifice to the Atlach Nacha, spinner in the darkness, weaver of dreams.

Appendix A. The World's Fair Hotel

"In all America there was none other like it . . . Its stairways ended nowhere in particular. Winding passages brought the uninitiated with a frightful jerk back to where they had started from. There were rooms that had no doors. There were doors that had no rooms. A mysterious house it was indeed—a crooked house, a reflex of the builder's own distorted mind. In that house occurred dark and eerie deeds."

—The Chicago Tribune

DON'T BELIEVE that I've ever heard someone say they wanted less art or fewer maps, and few things call for a set of maps like a story set in H.H. Holmes' World's Fair Hotel, aka The Murder Castle. The maps you'll find in the next few pages were created by Toby Lancaster of Dark Realm Maps. Toby's maps have been nominated for ENnie awards, and were integral in helping me visualize the structure that Holmes built to trap and dispose of his victims during his years in Chicago.

No one really knows exactly how many fell to Holmes' psychotic ways. Of the 27 murders he confessed to, nine were confirmed (several were patently false as the victims were still alive), and some accounts held that as many as 200 died at his hands. With that in mind it should be no surprise when I tell you that there are inconsistencies with the period accounts of the hotel.

In researching and writing *The Devil's City* and *Horror in the Windy City* I anticipated editorial changes would be needed. For one thing the hotel was enormous, and we just didn't have the room in the book, and as a map that will also be used in a game, rows and

75

rows of empty rooms with few distinguishing characteristics just aren't very interesting. I also knew that information on the second and third floors was thin.

The journalists from the era had drawn their own maps and affixed sensational names to the rooms contained within based on the accounts of others. This was literally the story of the century, and coming on the heels of Jack the Ripper everyone had an opinion on the secrets within the walls of Holmes' home. Toby did an excellent job compiling the rooms, finding consistencies, and using his skills as a cartographer to assemble a cohesive layout. You may find yourself asking if this a historically accurate account of the World's Fair Hotel, and I would say it is not. I don't believe that there is such a thing, but we have taken those elements, embellished some, polished a few, and created a map that can take you down the halls and into the chambers of the Murder Castle. And of course, Sara and I added the spiders.

Which brings us to a look behind the curtain into the process that Toby and I go through in drawing these places and writing these stories respectively.

In Toby's own words, "I am imagining being in the space and for this location it was more visceral than I had anticipated. Not literally nightmare inducing, as it is after all only a map, but more on a psychological level. How does a mind conceive of such things like trapping and harvesting of vulnerable young women?"

My own process isn't much different. The maps Toby created are the scene upon which I build the story and set the stage. My imagination takes me to those dark halls, and into rooms thick with the coppery smell of exsanguination. Once there I do my best to describe it, and bring you along for the, often unpleasant, ride. If I've done my job you're seeing over my shoulder, if not . . . at least you have Toby's wonderful maps to tell your own stories.

Castle Hotel Level 1

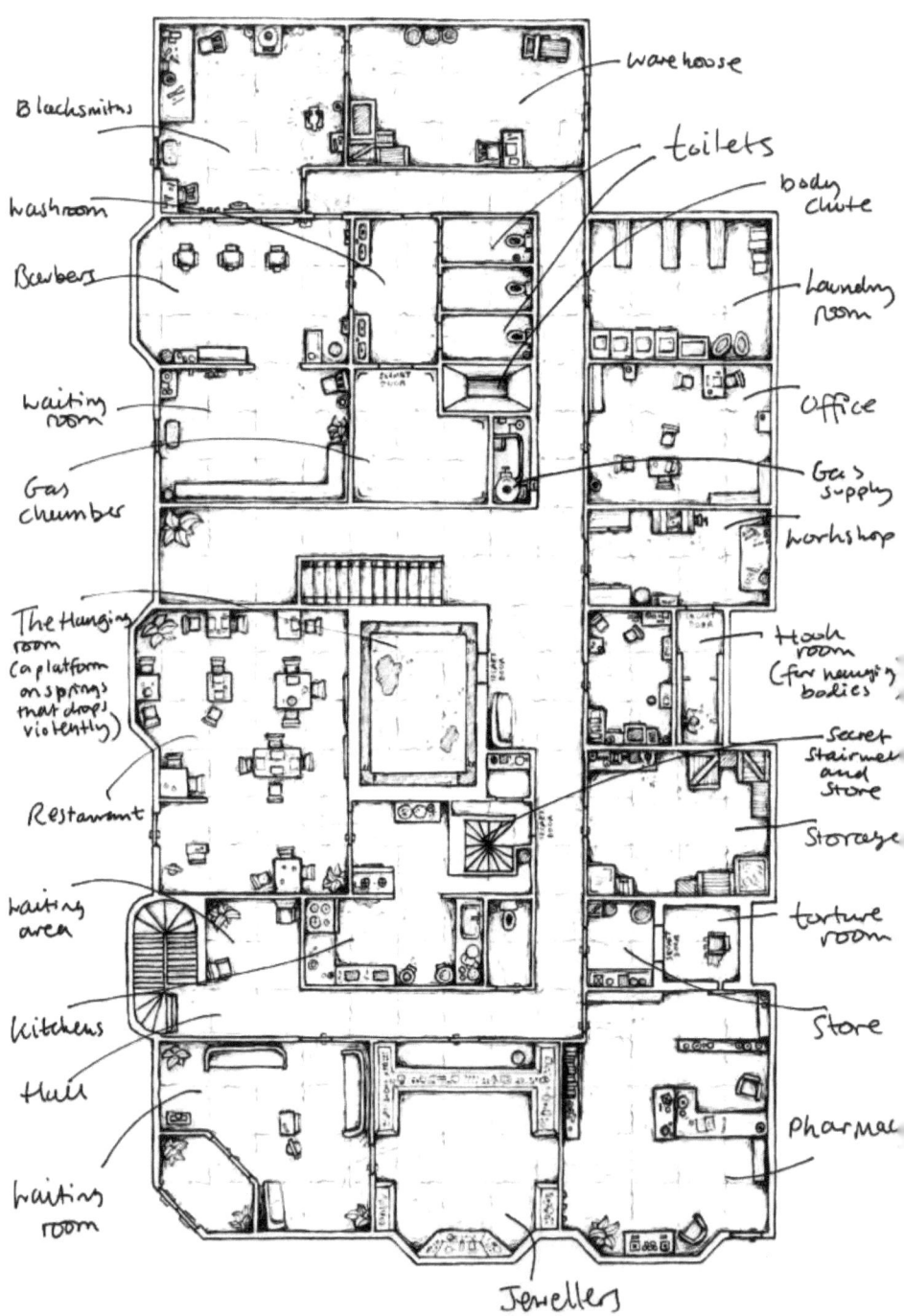

Warehouse

Blacksmiths

toilets

body chute

Washroom

Laundry room

Barbers

Office

Waiting room

Gas supply

Gas chamber

Workshop

The Hanging room (a platform on springs that drops violently)

Hook room (for hanging bodies)

Secret stairwell and store

Restaurant

Storage

Waiting area

torture room

Kitchens

Store

Hall

Pharmacy

Waiting room

Jewellers